Published exclusively for
Books for Children
P.O. Box 50
Leicester LE1 9AW
by Walker Books Ltd
184-192 Drummond Street
London NW1 3HP

First published 1986

Printed and bound by L.E.G.O., Vicenza, Italy

ISBN 0-7445-0510-0

opposites

By Ruth Thomson
Illustrated by Katy Sleight

WALKER BOOKS
LONDON

big

big parcels

Grandma sent Rosy Rabbit a big parcel.

But her cart was too small to carry it.

up

Rosy's friend Bella brought her cart.
'Heave ho!' she said. 'Lift the parcel up.'

'Now put it down gently. There we are.'

back

'I'll go at the back and push,' said Bella.

'I'll go at the front and pull,' said Rosy.
'Off we go.'

stop

'Stop at the red light,' Bella said.
'Look left and look right.'

'Go now the light is green.'

bottom

At the bottom of the hill they had a rest.

They also had a rest at the top
of the hill.

hot

Bella was hungry.
She bought a hot dog.

cold

cold
drinks

Rosy was thirsty.
She bought a cold drink.

over

'Not far now,' said Bella. 'Over the river...

under

and under the railway and we're home.'

shut

'Here's my house,' said Rosy. The gate
was shut. The front door was shut too.

Rosy went in. 'The gate is open now and so is the front door,' she said.

inside

Rosy went inside to clear a space.

Bella waited outside with the parcel.

wide

'Oh, no!' said Bella.
'The parcel is too wide.'

'The door is too narrow, you mean!'
said Rosy.

full

So Bella and Rosy opened the parcel in the garden. It was full of toys!

'Now it's empty!' said Rosy.
'What fun we'll have!'

And they did have fun! And so
did all their friends.

And you can have fun too – finding
all the opposites on these two pages!